JADED
and TYED

PENELOPE WARD

First Edition, April 2017
Copyright © 2017 by Penelope Ward
ISBN-13: 978-1544862613
ISBN-10: 154486261X

Editor: Elaine York, Allusion Graphics, LLC/
Publishing & Book Formatting, www.allusiongraphics.com
Cover Photo: Deposit Photos
Cover Design: Letitia Hasser, RBA Designs, rbadesigns.com
Interior Formatting: Elaine York, Allusion Graphics, LLC/
Publishing & Book Formatting, www.allusiongraphics.com

For My Peeps

PROLOGUE

Tyler

What the fuck was that?

Leaning against the bathroom door, I was sweating, trying to make sense of my reaction to a woman I'd never met before.

One minute, I was out buying beer to take back to my family's Christmas party. The next, I was losing my words, barely able to speak.

I don't react like that to women. They react like that to *me*. That was how it always worked.

I wasn't expecting that—to see her standing there when I got back to my brother's place.

Jade. My sister-in-law, Chelsea's, sister.

I'd heard about her, knew she was an actress on Broadway. Always thought that was funny, since I was a stage actor, too—albeit on a smaller scale. But I had never met her before, since she lived in New York.

But now she was here.

I was *quite* aware of that. My mind was aware of it. My pulse was aware of it. My dick was certainly aware of it. We were all quite aware.

1

I'd made an ass of myself, acted like a blubbering idiot, and fuck if I knew why.

What was it about her that made me forget my own name; made me clumsy?

She was gorgeous, yes. But there are plenty of gorgeous women out there. I'd certainly never had that kind of reaction to any of them.

This wouldn't have been so messed up if Nicole—my girlfriend—hadn't been standing right there, witness to it all. It was the epitome of awkward, particularly when I dropped one of the bottles while putting the beer away. The glass had shattered everywhere.

I cringed, letting out a deep breath as I leaned into the sink.

Just shake it off.

There was a knock at the door then my brother's voice.

"Dude, what the hell? I need to piss. Someone's in the other bathroom."

I opened and let him in. Damien immediately proceeded to whip his dick out and take a leak while he examined my face.

"What's going on with you?"

"Nothing."

After a long pause, he zipped up his pants. "Bullshit."

"Holy shit. How did you not tell me her sister was hot as fuck?"

"Is *that* what you're doing in here? Jerking off?" He squinted, examining my face. "What's wrong with you?"

"You didn't see what just happened out there?"

"What?"

"When Chelsea introduced me to Jade, I acted like a fucking idiot, became tongue tied. Nicole was standing right there. It was embarrassing. I don't know what the fuck is wrong with me tonight."

"So what? You're attracted to Jade. You made a fool of yourself for some God forsaken reason. That's what happened. Let it go."

"She's beautiful, yeah. But I don't really get why she had such an effect on me. I just lost it for a bit."

"Your inner teenager came out. It probably doesn't mean anything. I'm relieved you're with Nicole, to be honest."

"Why's that?"

"Because if you were single, you'd be trying to get into Jade's pants. I know you. If you ever fucked around with my wife's sister and ended up breaking her heart, that would *kill* Chelsea. I'd therefore have to kill *you*." He paused. "Where's this all coming from, anyway? You seem happy with Nicole. You've been with her a year. You love her, don't you?"

I've told her so, yes. But...I just don't know for sure.

"Yeah...I think so...I mean..."

Damien lifted his brow. "You're hesitating."

"We tell each other we love each other, alright? But how do you *really* know if you love someone? Is there a barometer for that?"

"I'm not sure this is a conversation we should be having in the bathroom with her right outside."

I insisted, "Just answer me. How did you know you loved Chelsea?"

3

Without hesitation, he said, "It was when I realized that I would die for her. When someone else becomes more important than your own life, that's how you know. Coming to that realization was an eye opener."

"Hmm."

"Would you die for Nicole?" When I seemed to take forever to answer, he shook his head and said, "Wow. You wouldn't."

"How do you know that?"

"Because you shouldn't even have to think about it."

Pondering that, I was speechless. That had never occurred to me, but it made a lot of sense.

Damien opened the door. "I gotta go back out. You'd better follow soon."

"Alright. Be right there."

By the time I made my way back to the living room, Nicole was sipping eggnog and immersed in a conversation with my mother. She winked at me, seemingly unaffected by my unusually long absence. Relief poured over me that she didn't seem pissed about my weird behavior earlier.

Good.

This is good.

All seemed right in the world again until my eyes wandered to the other corner of the room. The adrenaline started to build again when my gaze landed on Jade.

Her big, beautiful eyes. Her cute, little nose. Her long, slender neck. Her legs went on for days; she was almost as tall as me. I shunned away visions of those long legs wrapped around my waist.

Stop.

She was so animated—captivating. The light in her eyes was practically blinding. Jade was totally driving the conversation she was having with some friends who'd just arrived. This girl likely owned any room she was ever in.

At one point, she glanced over and noticed me watching her. My instinct was to look away, but I didn't. I brazenly kept my eyes on hers; I selfishly wanted those five seconds. Because I knew it was basically all we could ever have. It didn't mean anything. What I was feeling for her was just some unexplained, instant primal attraction.

She lived in New York anyway. Not to mention, I was in a committed relationship. And even if those two things didn't exist, I knew I could never trust myself with Chelsea's sister. I would inevitably fuck up. She was family. I needed to treat her like I would treat any family member. That meant not fucking with them.

Or, well...not *fucking them*. Period.

I made it through the rest of that evening without making an ass of myself.

Over the next year, Jade and I wouldn't cross paths again—until one night when a surprise notification lit up my computer screen.

CHAPTER *one*

Jade

I was done.

Completely done with him.

As if my life hadn't been stressful enough lately, I found out that unbeknownst to me, I'd been dating a married man. Not only that, I couldn't just cut ties with him, because we were costars. I'd have to continue to face him day in and day out.

Jeremy had sworn that he and Karen were divorcing, that he'd moved out of their apartment. I truly believed him. Then again, he's an actor, right? So, maybe I should've known better.

Well, tonight, Karen decided to show up after our evening performance to surprise him for their anniversary. Apparently, everyone but me knew they were really still together.

What a disaster.

I couldn't bear to talk to anyone tonight, not even Chelsea, because then I would have had to talk about it. Drowning it all out sounded a heck of a lot better than rehashing everything.

I poured myself a rum and Coke and sat on the couch just staring into space for a while.

After an hour or so, I finally calmed down a bit and opened my laptop. I knew exactly where I was headed first. It was like a compulsion that had to be satisfied every time I went on social media.

Stalking Tyler Hennessey's Facebook page was my guilty pleasure.

Ever since that odd exchange between us last Christmas, I couldn't get my brother-in-law, Damien's, super hot, younger brother out of my mind. I couldn't even really admit my slight obsession to Chelsea because a.) Tyler had a girlfriend, and b.) What was the point anyway? We lived on different coasts, and honestly it was better off if we didn't mess with each other, since our siblings were married. Things would be really awkward if it didn't work out. And it *wouldn't* work out...because we were both actors. I couldn't think of a worse combination for a relationship: two actors. Case in point, what just happened between Jeremy and me. Actors couldn't be trusted. For the most part, they were egotistical and very good manipulators.

But knowing all of that didn't stop me from wanting a window into Tyler's world. I didn't understand it, but looking at him made me feel good. Sadly, it was his girlfriend, Nicole, who posted most of the pictures. She would tag him, and since his profile was set to public, I could see everything, even though we weren't technically "friends."

For some reason, Tyler intrigued me. Maybe it was his adventurous spirit. There were pictures of him and

Nicole ziplining in Costa Rica. He was also really sweet with our nephew. Nicole posted a picture of him the other day where he had Little Damien on his shoulders. It made me sad because I didn't get to see my godson whenever I wanted. Tyler had the liberty to just pop over to Chelsea and Damien's house in minutes. I envied that because I missed my family so much. I also particularly liked that photo because with Tyler's hands over his head, you could see his rock-solid abs peeking from under his shirt and the very top of his underwear. God, that was hot. With his dark hair, light eyes, and tanned skin, he was a beautiful man.

I had every photo of Tyler etched into memory, often going back to my absolute favorites and examining the details.

Can you see why I couldn't exactly admit my obsession to anyone? It was my dirty little secret. The fact that no one knew also helped convince me that it was harmless.

Tonight, I noticed that he'd posted a status about getting the lead role in a new show at the Bay Repertory. He added a new photo of himself and the director. His hair was a getting a little longer. I zoomed in on the photo to get a better look at his blue eyes and beautiful jawline. Tyler had also changed the banner at the top of the page to a promo graphic for the show. When I went to click on the picture to make it bigger, I accidentally hit *"Add Friend."*

My heart started to pound.

No.

No

No!

I didn't want to do that!

Before I could go back to reverse the action, something else happened.

He'd accepted my request.

Shit!

He must have thought that was really random of me. Even though our siblings were married, we had barely ever spoken. To receive a random friend request from me a year after the one time we'd met must have seemed odd—like I'd been thinking about him. *Stalking* him.

I know what you're thinking. Don't say it.

I was just about to close down my laptop in shame when a message notification chimed.

Tyler: Hey, Jade.

Type something.
Type.
Okay...uh...
Sound casual.

Jade: Hi.

Tyler: Long time no see. How are you?

Jade: I'm well.

Well, that was a lie.

Tyler: Good.

I think the rum and Coke might have been kicking in when I typed the next line.

Jade: That was a lie.

Tyler: What?

Jade: Things are actually pretty sucky.

Tyler: I'm sorry to hear that. My day sucked, too.

Jade: I bet I have you beat.

Tyler: Only one way to find out. What happened to you?

Jade: I found out I was dating a married man.

Tyler: Yeah. Okay. You win.

Jade: LOL.

Tyler: That is far worse than forgetting to record The Walking Dead.

Jade: You probably think my friend

requesting you is really random. It was actually an accident since the button is so close to the cover photo.

It took me a minute to realize my mistake. *Shit!* How could it have been an accident if I was on his page in the first place? Now, I'd made myself look like a stalker. *(Don't say it.)*

Tyler: So, you were just on my page lurking, and you accidentally hit the friend request button? LOL.

Jade: Actually, I was checking your page to see if there were any pictures of Little D that I'd missed.

I thought that was as decent attempt at a save.

Tyler: Ah. Thanks for explaining. I'd almost fucked up and admitted that I sometimes check Broadway.com to see what you're up to, but that would make me look like a stalker if it was one-sided.

Jade: You do?

Tyler: Maybe.

Jade: See anything interesting?

Tyler: You were at some party wearing a black dress that was held up on the sides by these giant, gold paperclips.

Jade: LMAO. It was vintage couture.

Tyler: It was...something. Yeah.

Jade: What else did you see?

Tyler: You were standing next to some older-looking dude in glasses.

Jade: Yes. That's him. The asshole, Jeremy.

Tyler: First rule of thumb in our business is never date a costar. They don't teach you that on the Great White Way?

Jade: It should be common sense. I guess you're smarter than me, Tyler.

Tyler: Not really. I learned the hard way. LOL.

Jade: Ah, I see.

Tyler: Yup.

Jade: Your girlfriend now...she's not an actress, though, right? Chelsea mentioned she does makeup?

Tyler: Yes. She's a freelance makeup artist.

Jade: Fun.

Tyler: "Fun." You really mean that, or you're just saying it?

Jade: Actually, that job sounds pretty boring. I wouldn't have the patience.

Tyler: That's what I thought. You don't have to sugarcoat stuff with me, Jade. We're family, remember?

Jade: Oh, yeah. Right. So much so, we've never even really had a conversation until now. LOL

Tyler: It's not my fault you've been stalking my page without so much as a hello. ;-)

Jade: I wasn't.

I totally was.

Tyler: I'm kidding.

Jade: Anyway, I'm probably taking up too much of your time.

Tyler: Not at all. I'm the one who interrupted your lurking with a message, remember?

Jade: That's true, I suppose.

Tyler: Hey, how's your mother?

The abrupt change of subject hit me hard. I didn't even know how to respond. My mother was diagnosed with stage four cancer six months ago. She'd been undergoing chemo in a feeble attempt to contain the disease that had already spread.

Living far away during this time had been the most difficult thing I'd ever had to do. But Mom insisted that it would upset her if I left New York to come home to California. She made me promise not to give up this role. But each day, not being there for her was eating away at me more.

Hot tears were streaming down my face.

Jade: She's not doing too well, actually.

Tyler: God, I'm sorry.

He must have sensed something when I didn't respond after a full minute.

Tyler: I didn't mean to upset you.

Jade: It's okay. I just can't really talk about it. The only way I'm able to survive this day to day is to pretend it's not happening.

Tyler: I can completely relate to that.

Jade: How so?

Tyler: The time period right after my father died. I was only eleven. It was easier to try to take my mind off things than to deal with it. Damien started doing graffiti. That was his way of handling it. That was when I first got into acting in middle school. It helped. The thought of losing someone who you love is unbearable, so it's just easier to block it out. I get it.

Jade: Sometimes I feel really selfish for being here. My sisters are the ones having to help take care of her while I'm across the country.

Tyler: Yeah, but like you said, your mother would be upset if you left. You're doing what she wants. She probably doesn't want you seeing her suffer, either. Don't feel guilty about anything. She's proud of you. She wants you to do your thing. That makes her happy.

His words had definitely given me comfort.

Jade: Thank you.

Tyler: No need to thank me.

Over the next several minutes, I kept typing sentences and erasing them, unsure of what to say next. I just knew I had never wanted anything more than to keep this chat going. I'd been miserable for weeks, but for some reason, talking to Tyler was making it all better.

Tyler: You typing up a dissertation there?

Jade: What do you mean?

Tyler: All I see are those little dots. It seemed like you were typing a lot.

Shit.

Tyler: Something you want to say?

Jade: To be honest, I'm not sure what to say next. I just know I'm enjoying chatting with you.

Tyler: You don't have to say anything compelling. I'm enjoying just shooting the shit with you, too. I've had this idea of you in my head, and so far you're nothing like it.

Jade: What idea was that?

Tyler: Just a preconceived notion of what a Broadway actress would be like.

Jade: You thought I was full of myself?

Tyler: I guess I was afraid of that, yeah. You're a little intimidating.

Jade: That's funny, because you're actually the one making ME nervous right now.

Tyler: I can sense that. And I can't even believe you just said that, by the way.

Jade: Why?

Tyler: Do you not remember the first time we met?

Jade: I remember.

God, how could I forget?

Tyler: When I forgot how to speak?

Jade: Yes.

Tyler: When I fucking broke that beer bottle?

Jade: Yes. LOL.

Tyler: It was because YOU made me nervous.

Jade: Why?

Tyler: I still don't understand it. That had never happened to me.

Jade: I guess some things are just inexplicable.

Tyler. Yeah. They are.

I was staring at the screen, still unsure of what to say but positive of my not wanting this conversation to end.

Tyler: Wanna know the truth?

Jade: Yes.

His next message floored me.

Tyler: I thought you were the most beautiful woman I had ever seen.

CHAPTER *Two*

Tyler

Well, that was a fucking stupid thing to say.

Dickhead!

She wasn't responding. Great. Why the fuck did I just admit that again? Oh, yeah, because I'm a fucking idiot.

Totally inappropriate.

I fisted my hand and bit on my knuckles as I watched the little dots dancing around as she typed. She was either unsure of how to respond to my asinine admission or was about to tell me to go fuck myself.

Jade: Well, if you saw me now, you wouldn't think so.

Phew. Alright, she's attempting to make light of it.

Tyler: Why? What are you wearing?

What are you wearing?

Seriously? Fuck. There I go again.

Quick. Make a joke.

Tyler: Can I just ask…whatever it is, does it involve giant, gold paper clips?

Jade: They were safety pins, not paper clips! And no, it doesn't. LOL. Actually, it's a pretty ugly scene here tonight. I've got my leopard print Snuggie on because my apartment is freezing. I was too tired to take my makeup off, so I have raccoon eyes, and I just spilled a little rum and Coke on myself. And if I haven't yet sank to the lowest point in my life, I might have just licked it off the sleeve of my Snuggie.

Somehow, even with all of that said, I doubted she looked anything but freaking gorgeous.

Tyler: Okay…I didn't hear anything past Snuggie. Explain.

Jade: OMG…You don't know what a Snuggie is? It's a wearable blanket.

Tyler: Oh, I KNOW what it is. I'm just wondering what in God's name you're doing wearing one.

Jade: LOL. It's the best. I live in this in the winter. Saves so much on heat because it keeps me really warm.

Tyler: You're basically wrapping yourself up like an Eskimo to save on heat? Don't they pay you enough?

Jade: Not to live in this city, no.

Tyler: Well, if you're gonna wear a Snuggie, why not draw even more attention to yourself by making it leopard print. ;-)

Jade: My thoughts exactly. LOL!

I could practically hear her laughter through the computer screen. I knew she needed to laugh. That made me smile.

Tyler: By the way, I saw our nephew today.

Jade: How is he?

Tyler: He called me a dick.

Jade: OMG...I just literally spit out my drink.

Tyler: Careful. You wouldn't want to have to take that Snuggie to the dry cleaners. That would be embarrassing.

Jade: LOL. Okay...Little D is only a year old. There is no way he called you a dick.

Tyler: I swear to God. It was his first word. Chelsea was there and confirmed it. He looked straight into my eyes and said, "dick."

Jade: What did you do?

Tyler: I nodded and said, "Touché, little man."

Jade: That's too funny.

Tyler: It was.

Jade: How is my sister doing? I mean, I talk to her almost every day, but it's hard to gauge if she's downplaying things to make me feel less guilty.

Tyler: She seems okay. I don't get to go over there as often as I'd like, but because I'm between shows now, I have a little extra time.

Jade: Congrats on the new role, by the way.

Tyler: How did you know about that?

Jade: The graphic you added as your Facebook cover photo.

Tyler: Oh, that's right. You were looking for pictures of Little D. ;-)

Jade: Sigh.

Tyler: LOL Thanks, though. It's no big deal. It's as good as I'm gonna get out here... until I reach the big time...like a certain someone.

Jade: Have you considered moving to New York? You can only go so far in theater living in northern California.

Tyler: Honestly, I have considered it, but it's hard to think about leaving my mother. She's had some issues for several years ever since my father passed. Damien has even less time now than he used to, so I'm not sure I could move far away from her. I know she would tell me to go and do whatever I needed to, but she's really more dependent on me than she realizes.

Jade: Well, can I tell you something honestly?

Tyler: I'd prefer you lie to me.

Jade: Are you always such a wiseass?

Tyler: Pretty much. What were you going to say?

Jade: New York is not all it's cracked up to be. Some days I wish I could just come home.

Tyler: You don't mean that. You wouldn't give it up. You're just frustrated because of that douche, and homesick on top of it.

Jade: You think so, huh?

Tyler: Yes. Part of the problem is that you're so far away from home. I bet if your family were in New York or if you were closer, you wouldn't feel that way.

Jade: You're probably right.

There was a pause in our interaction until her next message.

Jade: I miss my mom.

It killed me to hear her say that. I knew exactly what she was thinking, that she might not get to see her again if something happened. I could sense that she must have been crying.

Tyler: It's okay to cry.

Jade: How did you know?

Tyler: Intuition, I guess.

Jade: That's pretty freaky.

Tyler: Well, I'm a bit of a freak.

Jade: LOL

Tyler: ^^^You're laughing now.

Jade: Tyler Hennessey, don't you have somewhere to be tonight, other than talking to me?

There were a million things I was supposed to be doing. None of them were going to get done until she ended this conversation.

Because there was no way I was going to be the first to let go.

Tyler: I have all night, Jade.

Jade: Where is your girlfriend?

Oh, that's right. You have a girlfriend, fuckhead. Don't forget that. Thank you for the reminder, Jade Jameson.

Tyler: She's working right now, actually. She took a bartending job to supplement the makeup artist gig. I actually manage the restaurant where she works, but I'm off tonight.

Jade: That's right. Chelsea mentioned that you're a restaurant manager.

Tyler: Yup. The Bay Repertory stuff doesn't exactly pay the bills. What else did Chelsea tell you about me?

Jade: Nothing bad. She actually mentioned how helpful you were to her back when Damien and she were having issues early on. She thinks you're a sweetheart.

Tyler: She's a sweetheart, too. Seriously. The best thing that's ever happened to my family.

Jade: That's really nice of you to say. I feel

the same way about Damien. I'm so happy that my sister finally found the one.

Tyler: You'll find the right one, too, someday.

Jade: I thought I did once.

Tyler: What happened?

Jade: It's too long of a story to get into. Summed up in five seconds? His name was Justin. He was a musician. I thought he loved me. He broke my heart. But basically, it wasn't meant to be.

Tyler: Then along came the married snake...

Jade: That one was my fault. We had really strong chemistry on stage, and I foolishly believed that would translate into real life somehow. But he was married for the majority of the time I'd known him, so I ruled it out. I would never dream of becoming the other woman. So, recently, when he told me he was divorcing, I somehow fell for it. And one night at my apartment, one thing led to another. Two weeks later, I find out it was all a lie. He's been married all along. I'm so stupid.

28

I didn't even know him, but I wanted to kill this asshole.

Tyler: You're not stupid. He fucking lied to you. He took advantage of your vulnerability.

Jade: Yeah, but I thought I had better intuition.

Tyler: Jade, for what it's worth, with everything going on with your mom, you have a lot on your mind at this point in your life. You're probably not thinking straight. You shouldn't be so hard on yourself. You'll learn from it. It's okay to have moments of weakness. People make mistakes.

I'm pretty sure I might be making one right now.

Over the next few weeks, I tried to convince myself that my secret chats with Jade were nothing more than friendly banter. But I knew better. In reality, I was likely headed to hell in a handbasket.

The surge of adrenaline whenever the Messenger notification would pop up was proof that, deep down, this was much more to me than just a friendly message chain.

I wasn't expecting this to happen.

I *lived* for her messages—fucking addicted to talking to her.

And I was hiding in order to do it. There was no place I preferred being lately other than holed up in my room or in the bathroom talking to Jade.

If there was nothing wrong with it, why would I have to hide it whenever Nicole was home? Sometimes, I'd pretend to have to run an errand just so I could message Jade from my car in peace.

I knew it was wrong, but I'd managed to convince myself that it wasn't cheating, since there was nothing sexual involved. Emotional, maybe, but not sexual. Aside from that first night when I stupidly admitted my physical attraction to her, we'd kept things pretty platonic. I vowed that wouldn't change; I still maintained that I didn't want to ever get involved with Chelsea's sister. The distance between Jade and me was the blessing in all of this. She would always be in New York, and it was looking more and more likely that I was on the west coast to stay.

She and I really did just *talk*. We'd talk about our days, life goals, her past relationships. We talked about her mother. *A lot*. Her sisters. My brother. We talked about our nephew—we'd argue about whether he looked more like my side or hers. We'd discuss theater stuff, compare how things were managed in each of our shows. We could have talked shop all day long. We'd occasionally discuss politics, and sometimes that would result in little arguments, which I fucking loved. I loved fighting with her.

Sometimes, we'd talk about serious stuff, and other times, we'd just rehash what we'd eaten on a particular day. All of this, and I hadn't even heard her voice. It didn't matter. I loved communicating with her this way. What started as one quick message as a result of my curiosity had seriously turned into an unexpected friendship. Jade was nothing like you would assume based on her looks and occupation. She was down-to-earth, self-deprecating, and funny as hell. *So funny.*

For a very long time, I really did think that I was meant to be with Nicole. Now, I was confused. Even in the early days of my relationship with her, our conversations never ran as deeply as the ones I'd had in the short time I'd been chatting with Jade. It was hard not to compare them. I really needed to figure out what was going to happen with my girlfriend. It was getting to the *shit or get off the pot* level.

Nicole had made it very clear to me that she wanted to get married. She was constantly dropping hints. She and I had invested a lot of time into our relationship. That alone made me want to make it work. What was the point of the past two years if we were just going to give up now? And I didn't want to hurt her. It seemed a heck of a lot easier to just continue doing what we were doing. But then Damien's question from last Christmas would constantly come back to haunt me. *Would I die for Nicole?* I still couldn't answer a yes to that question with absolute certainty.

Add to that, my current dilemma—the fact that it was getting harder to keep thoughts of Jade at bay—and I was one confused motherfucker. Especially since *acting* on things with Jade wouldn't be an option. So, why would I change anything about my life if I couldn't really be with her?

On this particular night, it had actually been a couple of days since I'd last heard from Jade. I guess we were taking an unofficial break from communicating. Maybe that was for the best.

I was grateful that Nicole and I were headed to Damien and Chelsea's for dinner tonight. It would help take my mind off things. I just needed a mental break from worrying about my relationship. My brother, his wife, Little D, and the dogs would be a great distraction.

Nicole walked into the bathroom as I was spraying on some cologne. "Ready to go?"

"Yeah." I looked her up and down. "You look nice."

"Thanks, babe." She smiled.

Nicole was wearing a cute little dress and had her hair down. She had gorgeous, long, dark hair—the polar opposite of Jade.

Why am I thinking about Jade again?

"Are we bringing something?" she asked.

"Yeah. I'll stop on the way and get some beer."

She leaned against the doorway. "It'll be nice to see Little D."

"Yeah. He's getting big fast."

She crossed her arms. "Everything okay with you?"

I looked at her through the mirror. "Yeah. Why do you ask?"

"You've just been a little quiet lately. Is something up?"

32

Even though that should have been my cue to start a conversation about the state of our relationship, I chickened out.

"Everything is fine, Nic. Everything is great."

Like I said...hell in a handbasket.

The ride to Damien's was uneventful. The tension in the air between Nicole and me had lessened. We stopped for beer and picked up stuff to make frozen margaritas since Chelsea had mentioned we were having Mexican for dinner when I called to ask her what we could bring.

It was a breezy evening in San Francisco, and I felt unusually relaxed. I should have known that it was all too good to be true.

Chelsea opened the door, and before I could get the words out to greet her, it was like the wind got knocked out of me.

Behind her shoulders, I could see the beautiful, statuesque blonde standing in the corner of the room. It was déjà vu all over again. My heart started to beat out of my chest, not only because I'd nearly forgotten how stunning she was in person, but because there was a random guy also standing next to her.

Jade and I hadn't told anyone that we were connecting online; we'd agreed to that. So, I knew I was going to have to put on my acting hat real fast.

Damien must have sensed something about my reaction because he smirked at me.

"You remember my sister, Jade," Chelsea said.

I approached her and held out my hand, sounding unnaturally formal. "Yes, of course. How have you been?"

She swallowed as I squeezed her fingers. "Good."

I couldn't help the bitter undertone as I looked to her left and asked, "Who's this?"

"This is Craig."

He held out his hand. "Hey. Nice to meet you."

I offered a single nod. "Hey."

Nicole was the first to speak next. "It's nice to see you again, Jade."

Jade looked uncomfortable. "Same here."

"Are you staying long?" I asked.

"Our mother's condition took a turn for the worse. I couldn't stay in New York any longer. I asked for a leave of absence."

How come she didn't tell me?

I wanted to ask her that so badly but couldn't. Our eyes locked, and I knew she could sense my question, even though I hadn't verbalized it.

"I'm sorry to hear that," Nicole said.

"I really wasn't expecting to come home so soon, but I needed to be with her."

Nicole leaned against me. "I totally understand that. You won't regret that decision."

Jade looked like she was about to tear up, and it was fucking breaking my heart. I wish I could have gotten her alone for just five minutes. More than that, I wish I knew who the fuck this ginger-haired guy was.

The mood was very somber during dinner. I knew Chelsea and Jade's mother wasn't doing well, but I guess I didn't realize just *how* bad it was.

Jesus Christ, I had no appetite but forced the food down just to distract myself from looking at her. Her eyes were filled with sadness. Her flowery scent from across the table was driving me mad.

My chair skidded against the floor as I got up to head to the bathroom. I couldn't help myself. I opened up Messenger and typed.

Tyler: Why didn't you tell me you were coming?

I knew she might not have been able to answer me, but the question had been killing me. There was so much I needed to know, namely, whether she was dating Craig. I knew I had no right to be jealous, but damn it, I was. And that was really fucking eye opening.

When I returned to the table, she was staring straight into my eyes, and I knew that she'd read the message when she mouthed, "I'm sorry."

"Don't be," I mouthed back. I'd sincerely meant that. Making her feel guilty for not telling me she was coming was not my intention. She had way more important things going on and shouldn't have had to feel like she owed me an explanation.

After she got up to go to the bathroom, I could feel my phone vibrate. I knew she'd sent me a message. My heart was once again palpitating. Beads of sweat were forming on my forehead because being unable to read it was killing me. This was not a normal reaction to have to a message from your "friend."

Even though my feelings had been developing over the past several weeks, it was only at this moment that I came to a realization. Emotional cheating felt even more destructive in some ways. The lack of physical contact meant there was no way to let everything out. It was all pent-up. It was like a constant, looming rainstorm that would never develop. Without the downpour, it was never able to pass. It was just always there, like an ever-present hint of thunder in the distance.

And I was waiting for lightning to strike.

CHAPTER
Three

Jade

I leaned against the bathroom sink and typed.

> **Jade: It was truly a sporadic decision. My friend, Craig, agreed to accompany me so I didn't have to fly upset and alone. The understudy is gonna take my role indefinitely until I get back. I'm here for the long haul.**

I didn't think he'd be able to respond, so it shocked me when those little dots appeared about a minute later.

> **Tyler: I've been worried about you. I'm glad you're home.**

> **Jade: Me too. It was time.**

> **Tyler: Who's Craig?**

Jade: I've known him for years. He's like a brother to me. We've been in a few shows together, but I met him early on after moving to the city. He's originally from Sacramento. He's headed there tomorrow to visit family then flying back to New York in a few days.

Tyler: Where are you staying?

Jade: Here at Chelsea's.

Tyler: Okay.

Jade: Where are you messaging me from right now?

Tyler: The kitchen.

Jade: You should go back to the table.

When I returned, I saw he'd done just that. Nicole was leaning her head against his shoulder. It killed me to see him with her, even though I had no right to feel that way. Tyler had no clue how strong my feelings for him had become. I didn't tell him I was coming home for the sheer reason that I was hoping not to see him right away. I knew I wouldn't be able to handle that on top of everything else. I guess I should have known better than to think I could hide from him when we were—in his words—practically family.

Now, having to sit across from them while she was leaning into him was a harsh reminder of what I'd been trying to avoid.

I made small talk with Nicole throughout dinner, which was extremely awkward for me. Thankfully, Craig saved the day when he began telling stories from the early days of our theater careers.

Tyler had snuck looks at me all night, and the tension in the air remained thick.

By the time he and Nicole finally left, I was emotionally spent.

My sister snuck up on me as I was pouring the last of the wine into my glass in the empty kitchen.

"What's wrong?" she asked.

"What do you mean?" I took a sip.

"I can tell something is up with you."

It was truly impossible to lie to Chelsea. She was my one confidante, and I could always tell her anything. But Tyler and I had promised each other we wouldn't discuss the fact that we'd been communicating. Nevertheless, I could feel myself breaking down.

"Where is Damien?" I asked.

"He's taking a quick shower."

"If I tell you something, you have to promise not to tell him."

"Why?"

"It involves Tyler."

Over the next several minutes, I proceeded to tell her the entire story of how Tyler and I first started talking and how we'd grown closer, well, as close as two people could become being thousands of miles apart from each other.

Chelsea seemed upset with me. "I can't believe you've been hiding this from me."

"I'm sorry. It's just better if no one knows so they don't misunderstand what's going on."

"Misunderstand? I'm pretty sure I understand *exactly* what's going on." She shook her head slowly. "Holy shit... you're having an affair with Damien's brother."

Suddenly feeling flush, I shook my head. "It's *not* an affair. It's different."

"It's different, alright. It's called an *emotional* affair, except have you also seen the way he looks at you?"

"He won't leave Nicole. He won't."

"He told you that?"

"We've discussed the fact that the two of us could never actually date."

"Why is that, exactly?"

"For one, he lives here. I live in New York. But more importantly, he's like family, and it's too risky to get involved with someone you'll always have to see at family functions and so forth. But again...he has a girlfriend."

She lowered her voice. "Well, between you and me, I don't really see him ending up with her."

Even though I was desperate for it, I wanted to the smash the false hope that was brewing inside of me. "Why do you say that?"

"It's just a sense I get. She's a little superficial and fake. As much as he likes to portray himself as the flashy actor type, I think, deep down, he's more like Damien.

He wants to settle down, have the type of connection their mother and father had. Their parents were deeply in love before their dad died, you know."

"Are you forgetting that I'm not exactly wife material, Chels?"

"Says who? Your job is crazy, maybe, but you're one of the most loving, non-superficial people I know. Ironically, you're the *perfect* woman because you look like the type of person whom someone wants to have an affair with, but you're more the marrying kind at heart."

"Thanks...I think? Are you saying I look like a slut?"

Chelsea laughed. "No, I'm saying that most men with a pulse can't resist you. It's something I've observed my entire life."

"And that's gotten me into a lot of trouble lately. I'm done getting involved—even accidentally—with people who are taken. And I most certainly am not going to end up getting hurt by someone who still has feelings for another person. I don't want another Justin and Amelia situation. I won't be able to survive it. She even *looks* like Amelia. It drives me nuts."

Damien walked into the room. "Who's Amelia?"

We both turned at the same time to find him looking at us suspiciously. His hair was wet from the shower.

"No one," I quickly said.

"How was your shower?" Chelsea asked, trying to seem nonchalant.

"Well, I was nice and relaxed until I overheard my brother's name."

She tried to play dumb. "What do you mean?"

"Are you forgetting about my supersonic hearing?"

My sister sighed. "How much did you hear?"

"Enough to know that Tyler's about to get his ass beat."

Shit!

"He didn't do anything wrong," I insisted.

"Yet," Damien said.

"This is exactly why we never said anything about connecting online. We knew you'd misunderstand."

"Oh, I understand perfectly clearly. My brother has wanted to fuck you from the moment he first saw you. End of story. And as much as I believe that the two of you may even be compatible, I just don't trust his intentions right now."

"This isn't his fault. I was the one who contacted him. I...accidentally friended him on Facebook, and that's sort of how this all started."

Damien chuckled, "How do you *accidentally* friend someone?"

Chelsea placed her hand on Damien's arm. "Okay, I think we've done enough prodding for one night. Jade and Tyler are adults. I think it's best if we stay out of it."

He must have realized how upset this conversation was making me, because his expression suddenly turned serious. "I didn't mean to stress you out even more, Jade. It's hard for me to not slip into the big brother role when it comes to Ty, and now when it comes to you. You're both very important to me. In the end, it's none of my fucking business, and as long as he doesn't hurt you, he'll keep his nuts."

I couldn't help but crack a smile. "Thank you, Damien."

Late that night, as I sat up in bed in the guest room, my Messenger notification chimed.

Tyler: Hey...you awake?

Jade: I am. Hi.

Tyler: Hi. :-)

When I didn't write anything else, he typed again.

Tyler: I'm sorry if tonight was awkward.

Jade: Not at all.

Tyler: ...she says with sarcasm.

I'd been pondering the situation all night. The words were in the pit of my stomach. I needed to let them out.

Jade: I think it's best if we stop talking to each other. It just really hit me tonight that it's wrong to be keeping things from the people we love. You love Nicole. You shouldn't be talking to me every day

43

if she doesn't know about it. I haven't been thinking straight lately and have been acting against my better judgment. So, again, I think it's best if we stop our messaging.

There.

I said it.

Tears were pouring down my cheeks.

It wasn't what I really wanted. I didn't want to stop communicating with him. In fact, I felt like I needed him more than ever. But I knew this was the right thing to do. Tonight was proof that I was getting way too attached, and I needed to just rip the Band-Aid off.

It was taking him forever to respond.

Tyler: I don't know what to say, except that it's your decision. Just know that if you ever need to talk, I'm here.

CHAPTER *four*

Tyler

The rottweilers jumped all over me after I let myself in. Their barking echoed throughout the otherwise quiet space.

"Hey, Dudley. Down, boy. Hey, Drewfus. Okay...okay. I love you guys, too."

As Chelsea approached carrying my nephew, Little D pointed his index finger at me. "Dick!"

I rustled his curly, blond hair. "That's right. How's it going, buddy?"

I'd decided to stop by Damien's place since it was on my way home from rehearsal. I hadn't been there since the night of the Jade encounter.

"Where's Damien?"

Chelsea adjusted her grip on Damien Jr. "There's a leak at one of the apartments. He went to go take a look at it."

My brother owned the building where he and Chelsea lived. Occasionally, something would go wrong, and he'd always try his best to fix it himself before hiring outside help.

"I'm just going to put him down for his nap," she said. "Be right back."

As Chelsea walked my nephew to his bedroom, I took the opportunity to scope out the place. The room Jade would have been staying in was empty. She wasn't home. My pulse slowed after realizing I wouldn't be seeing her.

When my sister-in-law returned, I asked, "Where's Jade?"

"She's spent the last couple of days with my parents in Sausalito. Mom is doing worse, so it's best that one of us is there."

"I'm sorry, Chels."

She nodded silently then asked, "Everything okay with you and Nicole?"

Chelsea was acting strange, and I was now certain she knew something.

I lifted my brow skeptically. "Any particular reason you just asked me that?"

"No."

My sister-in-law was a horrible liar. It was one thing for Jade to keep things from her when they lived across the country from each other. But they were living together now. I was certain they had spoken about me.

"What exactly did Jade tell you, Chelsea?"

She blew out a breath in defeat. "Everything."

"Nothing happened."

"Really?" she asked incredulously.

After a long moment of silence, I said, "Well, there's nothing going on anymore. We haven't been in touch in weeks. That was what she wanted. But you probably already know that."

"It's not really what she *wanted*, but it's the way she feels it has to be."

The phone rang, interrupting our conversation. I could hear that Chelsea was talking to Jade.

"Jade...speak slower. I can't understand you." She blocked her ear with her finger to hear better. "I can't come get you now. I just put Little D down for his nap, and Damien is fixing a broken pipe in the building."

Suddenly, my heart started pumping.

I interrupted, "Does she need a ride?"

Chelsea covered the phone with her hand. "Yes. She's at my parents'. She's having a bit of a panic attack and was wondering if I could come get her. I think being there for two days straight has been a bit much for her. She doesn't have a car yet. Damien had dropped her off."

"Tell her I'm on my way. I'll just need you to text me where to go."

"Are you sure?"

"Yes."

She resumed talking to her sister. "Tyler is going to come get you." It was clear that Jade wasn't too happy about that when Chelsea again had to insist, "Jade...I'm *sending* him to get you. He's here anyway. He's on his way." She paused. "Okay, I'll tell him."

Chelsea ended the call, "She said to just beep the horn when you're out front and she'll come out. She doesn't want my dad to ask questions. I'll message you the address."

"Okay."

As strange as it was going to be to pick her up under these circumstances, I couldn't help the feeling of excitement in my stomach.

As I walked to my car, I remembered that I had something in my trunk that I'd bought to show Jade months back. My original intention was to take a picture of it and send it to her on Facebook. I never had the chance since she'd stopped communicating with me. But since I'd be seeing her today, I'd get to use it.

I wasn't sure if anything could cheer her up under the circumstances, but I was damn well going to try.

CHAPTER *five*

Jade

The door to my mother's room was closed. She was sleeping more and more lately as result of the morphine they'd been giving her to dull the pain.

The past two days had been a reality check. I felt even more guilty for all of the months I'd been away. But I needed a breather. It was too much to see her suffering like that.

My father came up from behind me as I stood wiping my tears by the window.

"I'm sorry, honey. I can only imagine how hard it is to see your mother like this. She's always been our rock, hasn't she?"

"I'm sorry I can't be stronger for you, Dad."

"Your leaving New York was a big sacrifice and showed tremendous strength. Just take care of yourself, pumpkin. That's all you need to worry about. This is equally hard on all of us."

"I'll be back tomorrow, first thing in the morning." I felt the tears forming again. Not wanting Dad to see me cry, I said, "A friend is picking me up. I'm gonna wait outside and get some air, okay?"

"Of course," he said as we embraced. "I love you."

"Love you, too."

Outside, the sun was beginning to set. I let the tears roll down my cheeks as I sat down on my parents' steps. Listening to the sound of my neighbor's wind chimes, I rested my head on my knees and cried harder as my tears wet the material of my leggings.

The sound of gravel under the wheels of a car caused me to look up. I quickly wiped my eyes as I spotted Tyler's black Ford Explorer pulling in.

As I stood up and approached him, I had to squint to be sure I was seeing things clearly.

Oh my God.

What the?

When he waved, I couldn't help but burst into laughter. I could no longer distinguish my happy tears from the sad ones.

He came around to open the passenger side door for me. In that moment, I happened to look up to find my father staring down at us from the window. I could only imagine what he must have been thinking: *What on Earth is Damien's brother doing picking up my daughter dressed in a zebra-print Snuggie?*

"What are you doing in that thing?"

"I thought you loved this look, Jade."

"In the privacy of my own home, yes."

When he came back around to the driver's side, he flashed a wicked grin. God, he was handsome. I never realized how his smile accentuated his dimples before. It amazed me that he could even look sexy in a freaking wearable blanket.

"Well, you succeeded in making me laugh, Tyler."

"Is that why your mascara's running?"

"I have raccoon eyes because I was crying before you got here. But now I'm not. So, thank you."

He turned on the car. "Where are we going?"

I wiped the corners of my eyes again. "I don't know."

His car smelled faintly like a mix of cigar and cologne. I loved it.

"You want me to take you back to Chelsea's?"

"Yeah, I guess so."

"You don't sound too enthused to go back there," he said as we drove away.

"I feel like I just don't belong anywhere at the moment, to be honest. My parents' house is depressing and sad, and Chelsea's place is like a zoo, between the dogs and Little D. I love them, but I'm just used to my privacy."

"You want privacy?"

"I don't think that's possible unless I check into a hotel."

He pursed his gorgeous lips and seemed to be pondering something. "I'll take you some place you can be at peace for a while."

"Where?"

"It's a little place I like to call...you'll find out."

Feeling too weak to fight him, I simply asked, "How did you get a Snuggie so fast, anyway? They're not that easy to find anymore."

"You should know, right?" He smiled. "I bought it a while ago, actually. I was going to send a picture of myself in it to you as a joke. But I never had the chance because you stopped talking to me."

"You know why I did it."

"I do. I don't blame you, even though I miss talking to you." He glanced over at me. "But you were justified. Just because something makes us feel good, doesn't mean it's right."

"So what is *this*...what we're doing right now?"

"I think you need a friend right now. Right or wrong... just let me be that for you tonight. We can go back to not talking tomorrow."

We kept driving down the 101 until he pulled off onto one of the exits.

"I'm just getting something for us to drink," he said. "You look like you can use one. Am I right?" He winked. "I'll be back."

I watched as he ran into the liquor store, still covered in the zebra blanket.

When he returned, he shut the driver-side door and turned to me, "Can you believe some people were staring at me like I was crazy?" he joked as he placed the paper bag of alcohol in the back seat.

"Well, they weren't expecting to see a zebra walk in."

"And one that's driving around a raccoon, at that!" he joked. "Quick! Someone call animal control."

Tyler managed to make me laugh again. I didn't question where he was taking me or what his intentions were as we continued to just drive.

Before I knew it, we had pulled up to a gray, stucco house in San Jose.

"Where are we?"

Tyler smiled. "This is my mama's house."

"Isn't she going to question why I'm here?"

"Nah. We're not going inside the main house anyway."

"Where are we going, then?"

"My treehouse. I'm gonna set you up in there. Then, I'll leave you alone."

"Is this treehouse stable?"

He chuckled. "What do you mean, stable?"

"Like...structurally sound."

"Spoken like a city girl. Yes, it's fine. This is a treehouse like no other. You'll be safe." He'd placed his hand briefly on my thigh when he said it, and the muscles between my legs instinctively contracted. I was so incredibly attracted to him, and perhaps hadn't realized just how much until this moment.

I cleared my throat. "I have a little fear of heights. That's why I asked."

"You're not going to be plummeting down. Don't worry."

"Good. Because that would make an already shitty day worse."

Tyler wasn't kidding. Once we'd climbed up, it was evident that this was no ordinary treehouse. It was state of the art with electricity, a full-sized bed, and even a television. He explained that his dad had started building it before he passed away. Eventually, Damien and Ty completed it.

He turned on the lamp and noticed me shivering. "You cold?"

"A little."

He lifted the long zebra blanket over his head. "Here, get in this."

Tyler approached and placed the fleece fabric over my head. The blanket was warm from his body and coated in his intoxicating smell. It was easy to imagine that it was him wrapped around me. My breasts began to tingle.

I wanted him.

His hair was tousled from having pulled the blanket over it. Now that I could see his body, I couldn't help but stare at Tyler's toned physique. His muscles were busting through his black, fitted shirt. His beautiful, blue eyes were glistening as he looked at me. They were definitely reflecting a reciprocal attraction. I could feel it, could practically taste it, and it was as uncomfortable as it was arousing. *Definitely more arousing.*

Yet, despite the sexually-charged energy in the air, there was also a sense of comfort. We already knew each other intimately from the many conversations we'd had. (Well, as intimately as you could know someone from Messenger.) But the physical awareness of actually being next to him was something I was certainly not used to.

I finally spoke, breaking the tension in the air. "How did you know I was missing my Snuggie? I left it behind in New York."

"I know you pretty well, Jade."

"Is that so?"

"Only because you let me in for a while."

I know.

That was dangerous.

He blinked, seeming to break his stare. "Anyway, make yourself at home. I'm gonna get you set up with a drink and then I'll get out of your hair if you want some privacy. There is no more peaceful place than up here, listening to the rustling of the leaves."

"What are you gonna do tonight?"

"Hang out with my mother, sleep in my old room. I'll take you back to Sausalito in the morning."

I asked the question that was the elephant in the room. "Does Nicole know where you are?"

He swallowed. "I texted her from the liquor store, told her I was spending the night in San Jose at Mom's."

"I see," I simply said.

Tyler took the alcohol he'd bought out of the crinkled paper bag.

"What are you serving tonight?"

"Whiskey sours. I bought the best whiskey, too." He winked.

"Hennessy. Very funny."

His mouth curved into a smile. "Actually, I prefer the taste of Jameson."

CHAPTER
six

Tyler

Jade's face turned red after I'd said that. I hadn't meant for my comment to sound so suggestive. But God, the thoughts that my words triggered.

I'm sure the taste of Jade Jameson is far better than any whiskey.

She cleared her throat. "Really...you prefer Jameson to Hennessy?"

"Yup. Hennessy is technically Cognac. I like whiskey better."

She smiled. "I remember thinking it was so funny when Chelsea first told me Damien's last name. She didn't know that Hennessy and Jameson were brands of alcohol."

"I could see that totally going over her head. It was the first thing I thought of."

"Me, too." She smiled and seemed to blush.

She looked uncharacteristically shy in that moment. Wrapped in the zebra blanket, her mascara was still smudged, and her lipstick was a little smeared. I imagined what it would have been like to kiss the rest of it off. My dick twitched at the thought.

She was so naturally beautiful that she didn't need any makeup. Her tiny nose was perfectly pointed. She had the biggest eyes, and in this moment the light that had been missing from them earlier had seemed to return. It pleased me to know that I was responsible for that.

"I'll be right back, Jade Jameson. I have to get you a glass from downstairs."

"Okay." She made herself comfortable on the bed and asked, "Are you gonna have some with me?"

"Maybe just one."

Just when I was about to make my way down, her voice stopped me. "Tyler?"

"Yeah?"

"Thank for you this...for tonight."

"My pleasure."

Once inside Mom's, I tried to be as quiet as possible, hoping she wouldn't notice me in the house. My mother was usually in her bedroom this time of night meditating or reading. No such luck tonight, though.

Her voice snuck up on me. "Tyler...I didn't expect to see you here tonight."

"Mom..."

"Why do you seem startled, son?"

"I just thought you'd be in your room."

"What are you up to?"

"Nothing."

Knowing I was lying, she tilted her head. "Tyler..."

A guilty laugh escaped me. "I was just grabbing a couple of glasses to take up to the treehouse."

"Is Nicole there with you?"

I paused. "No."

"Who's the second glass for?"

I hesitated then answered, "Jade."

She raised her forehead. "Jade...Chelsea's sister?"

"Yes."

A knowing look flashed across her face. "Oh."

We stared at each other for a few seconds until I said, "Nothing's going on. She was at her parents' house. With their mom doing worse, Jade had like a little breakdown. I happened to be at Damien's when she called Chelsea for a ride. I offered to pick her up since Little D was sleeping. Jade didn't want to go back to their house, so I brought her here instead. She's under a lot of stress, and I thought the treehouse would be a nice sanctuary."

"You don't need to explain."

"Why are you looking at me like that, then?"

She laughed a little. "Tyler, with all due respect, your reaction to that woman last Christmas has become legend. If you expect me to believe that there's absolutely nothing salacious about you hiding her in the treehouse right now, you're crazy."

"How did you know about what happened last Christmas? You weren't in the room when it went down."

"Your brother told me."

"Great."

My mother grabbed her tea kettle and started to fill it before she said, "There's nothing wrong with being smitten. We can't choose whom we're attracted to. But is there something more going on?"

I'd never had the ability to lie to my mother. Over the next few minutes, I explained to her what had been developing between Jade and me.

"Just be careful," she said. "I like Nicole. I do. She's very sweet. But I don't believe she's the one. Something has to be missing for you to have let things go so far with Jade. You're young. You have the right to change your mind. But you don't have the right to string someone along. No woman deserves to be with a man whose heart is with someone else."

She wasn't telling me anything I hadn't already known for a long time.

"You're right. But as long as I'm with Nicole, nothing will happen with Jade."

"By the same token, don't believe that you can't have something just because it feels too good to be true. You deserve perfection."

I needed to get back to Jade.

"Thanks for the talk, Ma." I started to walk away when she stopped me.

"Oh, Tyler?"

"Yeah?"

"Try not to drop the glasses." She smirked.

"Wiseass."

My heart raced as I climbed back up to the treehouse with the glasses in hand.

"That took a while," Jade said. She'd been lying on the bed and sat up.

"My mother caught me."

A flash of panic washed over her face. "You didn't tell her I was up here, did you?"

"I kind of had to. It's okay. She's cool with it."

"She thinks we're having an affair."

I nodded. "Pretty much."

Jade wasn't amused. "I don't want your mother to think I'm a bad person."

"She doesn't. I told her the truth."

She was quiet as I prepared her drink then handed it to her.

"Here."

She took it from me and tasted it. "Mmm. That's good. Burns a little going down. But it's just what I need." Taking another sip, she asked, "So when does your show start up?"

"In a month. We started rehearsals this week. I was coming from there when you called for a ride."

"You should probably be studying your lines tonight instead of babysitting me."

Her comment reminded me that I'd forgotten that I was supposed to be somewhere tonight.

"Hang on," I said as I typed out a text.

"Who are you texting?"

"I was supposed to meet my costar, Audrey, to practice this one scene tonight. I never told her I couldn't make it."

"I'm getting you in trouble."

You have no idea.

Audrey texted me back immediately. "She just responded. She says it's no big deal. Her husband will run lines with her."

"You want to practice the scene with *me*? I'll do Audrey's part."

Her question had caught me off guard.

"Are you serious?"

"Why wouldn't I be?"

"I thought you wanted privacy tonight. I was gonna head downstairs and just let you be."

"I really don't want to be alone."

Well, then we're both on the same page.

Leaving her was the last thing I wanted.

"Okay. I'll go to my car and get the script."

As I returned to the treehouse with it, a sudden self-conscious feeling came over me. What if she thought my acting was shit? After all, she was the real deal.

"So, you know the gist of the story, right?"

"You've told me bits and pieces. But tell me about this scene."

"My character, Xavier, is a writer who's trying to pen the next Great American Novel. His wife, Justine, is basically considering leaving him because she's feeling neglected. In this scene, she's confronting him about it."

I watched Jade as she intently read over the scene.

"Okay, I'm ready," she finally said.

Because we only had one script, I sat next to her on the bed so we could share it.

We started going back and forth, and I was blown away by how naturally she fell into the role. She was a true professional, and it showed. She read the lines with so much passion in her eyes, completely transforming into the character. It even looked like her eyes were watering. Although I suspected that might have had something to do with her current emotional state, I'd never worked with anyone who could cry on cue.

At one point, I stopped mid-scene. "You're amazing."

"That's not in the script."

"No, it's not."

A long moment of silence ensued.

"You know, I don't think you could ever pull off the role of Justine. You're too perfect-looking. Her character is supposed to be this flawed, ugly duckling."

She pondered my comment then said, "You know something? I've heard that line my entire life—that I'm too good-looking, too perfect. And, you know what? It's never worked out for me. Because, in the end, at the least as far as my past relationships have gone...the quirky, plain Jane gets the man. Once the excitement wears off with someone like me, they want to settle down with someone who's not so ambitious."

"Maybe you just haven't found a real man, one who can handle you."

I felt up for that challenge.

"The thing is...it's not that I don't want to be that girlfriend who stays home watching movies at night instead of performing...but I want it all. I want the family someday *and* the limelight. I don't want to settle for one or the other."

Her passion for life and ambition were partly what I loved about her.

"You deserve everything you want. You shouldn't have to settle. *Ever.* I can relate in that I'm sort of stuck between what I want for myself and what I feel I need to do for others. If I were really serious about acting, I'd have moved to L.A. or New York. I want a comfortable life near my family and friends, but I also crave more. *Much more.* So, I can relate to that anxious feeling. Like there's something bigger out there waiting to be had that I'm missing out on."

She smiled like she understood exactly what I was saying. "I think we're a lot alike that way."

"Yeah."

Our eyes locked for longer than normal.

Jade suddenly said, "It's getting really hot in here. I think I need a break from the zebra for a while."

Jade lifted the blanket over her head, revealing the thin, white shirt she was wearing underneath. Her erect nipples were peeking through. I couldn't help but stare for a few seconds. Maybe more than a few. I knew she was aware of how attracted to her I was. It was certainly no secret. But she couldn't have known just how much I wanted her in that moment. My dick stiffened, and I fought like hell to keep from getting hard.

I didn't know what came over me, but I was bursting with need, a need to tell her what I was thinking. The words left my mouth before I could think them through.

"I would leave her for you, Jade."

CHAPTER *seven*

Jade

Did he just say what I think he did?

Tyler continued, "I don't know how to say this... without coming across like a total dick. Despite what our nephew thinks...and even what Damien thinks of me sometimes, I'm really not a dick. I'm trying to be a better person than I used to be."

I appreciated his honesty, and even though it filled me with excitement, it made me more nervous than anything.

"Saying that you'll leave your girlfriend for me doesn't exactly give me the warm fuzzies. Who's to say that this won't happen again? Someone else will come along better, prettier than me...and history repeats itself."

Tyler momentarily gripped his own hair, looking like he was struggling to explain his feelings. "I didn't think I wanted anything else, Jade. I was happy—so I thought. I wasn't *looking* for you. If you want a logical explanation as to why I feel the way I do about you, I can't give you that. I can't explain what it is about you that causes me to lose my mind. I've tried to understand it. I just know that when I first met you, I thought you were the most beautiful woman in the world on the outside, but even that couldn't quite explain my reaction. Now that I've gotten to know you over time, I am certain that it's what's on the *inside* that's most beautiful. I'm crazy about you, but I don't know if you feel the same about me, because you've never told me. And it's a really shitty thing to say that I haven't left Nicole because I don't know if I can ever really have you, but that's the truth. I feel like a piece of shit for feeling the way I do, but I need to be honest with you. I want you to know that I have never felt this way about anyone."

Hearing him say that was as terrifying as it was amazing. "You scare me, Tyler."

"Why?"

"Because from the moment I first met you, I felt like you belonged to me in some way. I don't know whether it was because you're Damien's brother and I'm Chelsea's sister, and so it would make sense that we would be matched up or what...but I felt this unwarranted possessiveness from the moment we met. And obviously, that's a problem... because you're taken. I thought the feeling would just go away. But I couldn't stop thinking about you after that day. That was why I was on your Facebook page that first time we connected. But I just don't know how to do the long-distance thing or even know how to fully trust you. All I know is that when we're connecting, I feel differently than I do when I'm with anyone else. But I have to admit, it scares me, because I don't know if it could really work between us."

His eyes darkened. "Why do you doubt that?"

"Let's just assume Nicole wasn't even in the picture. Let's just look at you and me. I get almost no time off. You wouldn't want to leave your family and move to New York with no job. And then what if you got there and weren't happy? There are just a lot of unknowns, and honestly, Tyler, I don't know if I could ever stand to lose you. I know that sounds strange, but in other words, I can't lose you if I never have you in the first place. Does that make sense?"

He nodded. "It makes total sense. I don't want to ever be on bad terms with you, because I know we'll always be connected by our siblings' marriage. At the same time, I don't know how to be around you and *not* feel this way."

"What do we do?"

"There are only two choices. We do nothing...or we do *everything*. I don't feel like there's an in between with you, Jade. I feel like I went from zero to a hundred from the moment I first saw you."

He said he would leave her for me. But he didn't say what that meant. Would he move for me? Was it fair of me to even expect that he should, simply because I had the bigger career? Does he understand what the logistics of actually *being* together would even mean? Would he start to resent me if he decided to move? It was too much to figure out tonight.

As if he could read my mind, he said, "I'm sorry for blurting out what I did. I seriously don't know how to hide my feelings around you. You make me want to scream things out to you. I knew you'd have to come home to California eventually but never expected it so fast. When you were far away, it was easier. But I would never change having you here. I have a lot more to say, but this evening is about you relaxing. So, forget all the shit in your head, okay? I want you to rest, so I can take you back to your mother's house tomorrow with a clear mind."

I wasn't going to argue with that. It was safer if he left because I no longer trusted myself fully around him.

"Thank you, Tyler."

"Just text me if you need anything. I'll be right downstairs, okay?"

"Yes. Goodnight."

"Goodnight, Jade."

It was a peaceful rest of the night until the phone call that came shortly after 3AM.

CHAPTER *eight*

Tyler

My cell phone vibrating against the nightstand in my old bedroom woke me up.

It was a text from Jade.

Jade: My mother died.

Oh my God.

My hands were shaking as I bolted out of bed and headed toward the treehouse in the darkness of the night.

She was sitting on the bed, sobbing, with her head in her hands.

I'd never wanted anything more than to just take her pain away. Without thinking it through, I ran to the bed and wrapped my arms around her.

My heart was beating so fast. I knew that no words were going to help. She just needed me there.

I finally whispered, "Am I taking you home?"

"My father said not to come until morning."

"Okay."

She gripped my shirt. "I need you to stay. I don't want to be alone."

As if I could leave her.

"I won't leave you."

I positioned myself behind her in the bed as she rested the back of her head on my chest and sobbed.

Jade lay awake in my arms the entire night. It wasn't how I'd pictured holding her for the first time, but it was far more profound. I knew no matter what happened between us, I would never forget this night for as long as I lived.

It had been three days since that night with Jade. She needed to be with her family as they made the funeral arrangements.

But tonight, we'd be going to her mother's wake, so seeing her would be inevitable. Nicole insisted on coming with me. There was nothing I could have said to stop her, although I wished I could've just gone alone.

I didn't know what I was expecting to see, but I was unprepared for the firestorm of emotions that would hit me upon the sight of Jade standing there in that black dress.

There was a long line of people waiting to greet the family. There were so many people crowding the room, but my focus was on her and only her. Jade's eyes were red, and she wasn't making eye contact with anyone. I knew she was in a tremendous amount of pain, perhaps even more so than the last night we were together. It had all probably really sunken in now.

Damien was by Chelsea's side. The oldest sister, Claire, had her husband, Micah, to lean on. Jade was by herself, and it was killing me. I wanted to be standing next to her and felt like I would have given my life in that moment to take her pain away.

The realization of that thought was jarring.

My conversation with Damien from last year replayed in my mind, the one where I asked him how he knew he loved Chelsea.

"It was when I realized that I would die for her."

The other night with Jade was a game changer. Not only had I gotten to hold her, but it was as if all of the conversations we'd ever had, all of the feelings I'd ever felt had pummeled me all at once, too. As she cried in my arms, I remembered thinking that being with her—whatever it took—was really the only choice. Tonight had only solidified what I already knew.

I was numb when my turn came to greet her in the line. With Nicole right behind me, I couldn't say what I needed to say, couldn't hold Jade the way I needed to. I offered her all I could, a brief embrace and a tight squeeze of her back. It was painful to let her go.

I couldn't do this anymore.

Being here was a reminder of how short life was.

As soon as the cold night air hit our faces outside of the funeral parlor, I looked over at Nicole and forced the words out, "When we get home, we need to talk."

The next few days were spent getting my things out of the apartment I shared with Nicole and moving them into my mother's in San Jose. As expected, Nicole felt completely blindsided by my ending things.

She had every right to feel that way. I had chosen not to tell her the true reason for the break up because I didn't feel that would have made it any easier. I simply let her believe that I didn't see things progressing into marriage for us, and that I felt it was better to end things now than to waste any more of her time.

She'd called me every name in the book, accused me of ruining her life, and smashed some things around. I took it all because a part of me really felt that I deserved it. I felt horrible, but not any worse than I had in keeping the relationship going while I was pining over someone else. It had to be done. Even if I never ended up with Jade, the fact that I could fall for her had to have meant that something was missing in my relationship with Nicole.

Moving back in with Mom was not something I wanted to be doing in my late twenties, but I truly hoped it would be temporary.

I hadn't had a chance to tell Jade I'd broken up with Nicole. I wanted to do it in person but didn't want to disrupt her grieving with her sisters and father in the hours following the funeral.

I checked in with her over Messenger, but the last couple of times she hadn't responded. I chalked it up to her needing to spend time with her family without interruption.

After four days, I couldn't take it anymore. I needed to see her, needed to tell her that I was a free man and could now fully be there for her in any way she needed me. I needed to let out all of the feelings I'd been holding back.

With adrenaline pumping through my veins, I knocked on Damien's door.

My brother opened. "Hey. What's going on?"

"I need to see Jade."

"Well, you're two days late. She went back to New York. I figured you knew that."

The dogs were barking so loudly, and it felt like my head was going to explode.

"No. She never said anything to me at all."

Chelsea walked in. "Actually, she didn't want you to know. She just wanted to leave."

My voice grew louder. "Why?"

"Being here was too much for her. Mom's passing really hit her hard. She needed to escape back into work."

"Why did she not want me to know?"

Chelsea looked pissed at me. "Seeing you with Nicole at the wake was hard for her. She just felt it best to go back east. I have to say, I agree. The situation with you was unhealthy, especially given the circumstances."

My blood was pumping. "Chelsea…"

"What?"

"She has it all wrong. You have it all wrong."

"What do you mean?"

"I've spent the past few days dealing with breaking up with Nicole and moving my stuff out. It's over. I thought I was giving Jade space to be with the family. If I thought she would leave so soon, I would've been here in a heartbeat."

"You broke up with Nicole, and you came here to tell her?"

"Yes. I came here to tell her a lot more than just that." I raked my fingers through my hair. "I can't believe she would just leave."

"Well, you have to understand...she believed the situation would go on the way it was. She couldn't handle it and needed to get back to her job."

I started to pace. "I need to go to New York."

"You do?"

Stopping in my tracks, I looked Chelsea dead in the eye. "I am so in love with your sister."

Damien looked stunned to hear those words come out of my mouth. "Whoa." His mouth curved into a huge smile.

I turned to him. "Why do you look so shocked?"

"I guess it's because...I truly believe it. I can see it in your eyes. I know I've been skeptical of your intentions with Jade from the start, but I have to say, I'm proud of the way you've handled yourself, ending things with Nicole first."

"You were so right. You can't possibly love someone if you're not willing to die for them."

Damien's smile grew bigger. "Wow. It's like that, then."

"Yeah...it's like that." Looking over at Chelsea, I said, "I need to get on a plane."

CHAPTER *nine*

Jade

California was one big blur.

As I sat in my cold apartment wrapped in my leopard-print Snuggie, I felt emptier here in New York than I ever had. Watching the raindrops pelting my window, I took a sip of wine and closed my eyes.

I missed home already.

But I had to escape the pain; the pain of seeing my dad so sad, the pain of longing I was feeling for Tyler.

My director was thrilled that I would be returning to the show. And I needed nothing more than to throw myself into work this week.

Seeing Nicole at the service was a reminder of just how easily I could have ended up devastated by Tyler. He never told me definitively that he would have been willing to move to New York. We never had a serious conversation about what being together would actually mean. I doubted he even really thought it through.

Still, I couldn't shake the need inside of me. The memory of what it felt like to be in his arms was all too clear. The protective way he held me and assured me that everything would be okay. I could have really used some of that right now.

A teardrop fell down my cheek. Just as I caught it with my tongue, there was a loud knock at the door.

A feeling of dread came over me because I didn't want to have to answer it dressed in my Snuggie.

When I opened the door, my heart nearly combusted at the sight of Tyler standing there. His black hair was drenched from the rain. Droplets of water covered his black jacket. His chest was heaving—as if he'd been running.

I gasped. "Oh, my God."

Before I could say anything else, his hands cupped my cheeks. His warm lips enveloped mine as he let out the longest sigh into my mouth as if he'd been racing thousands of miles, and I was the finish line. I wrapped my arms around his neck and pulled him into the apartment as our lips remained locked.

I'd had myself convinced that I was somehow better off away from this man, but breathing him in at the moment felt necessary for survival. The sound of a suitcase rolling in with him vaguely registered, although I refused to break from his delicious mouth long enough to look down. He hadn't said a word, but somehow I knew my life would never be the same again.

When he finally pulled away, he was out of breath. "I've wanted to do that for so damn long."

Once again, he'd turned my sad tears to joyous ones.

"What are you doing here?"

He kissed me firmly one more time before he finally spoke, "Right after your mother's wake, I broke up with Nicole—that same night. I couldn't do it anymore, knowing how I felt about you. It took a few days to get everything out of the apartment and stuff. I thought you were going to stay in town much longer. I went over to Chelsea's on Thursday night to tell you everything, to be with you, and they told me you were gone."

I gripped his jacket and pulled him in closer. "I'm sorry."

"Don't be. I'm not even going to ask you why you left without telling me, because I know you assumed that nothing would change. You underestimate my feelings for you, Jade. And honestly, I can't even explain it because you literally make me speechless. It's like nothing I have ever felt. When I was holding you the other night in the treehouse, I was silently telling you everything. You were in so much pain, and it physically hurt me. I never realized what it felt like to love someone so much that you wished you could take their pain for them. It only made me realize even clearer how much I love you."

A fresh wave of tears formed in my eyes. "I have been in love with you for a really long time, Tyler. I just couldn't let myself believe that you would leave her until it happened."

"I get it. But did you ever really think I could let you go?"

"I was afraid. Honestly, now that my mother is gone, the only thing I'm afraid of anymore is losing you."

CHAPTER *Ten*

Tyler

It felt like a dream to hear those words coming out of her beautiful mouth. Jade was the embodiment of perfection, and she was afraid of losing *me*. As if anyone else could ever satisfy me again.

I needed to show her just *how much* I was hers. I couldn't wait another minute to touch her, taste her, show her how much I loved her.

Without seeking permission, I lifted the Snuggie off of her body and nearly went into shock when I realized she wasn't wearing anything underneath but her bra and panties.

My cock was already hard as steel from our kiss, but I could literally feel it moving, desperately needing to be inside of her.

Jade pressed her smooth, lithe body against mine as she took of my wet jacket.

"Do you have any idea how long I've dreamt of this?" I asked.

"Since the Christmas before last?" she whispered as I began to devour her neck.

My body was shaking with need as I unsnapped her bra. Her breasts were larger than I expected for her thin frame. They were gorgeous, perky with deliciously erect nipples. *They were mine.* Bending over to suck them, I could feel my dick throbbing.

While I wanted to take it slow in theory, the visceral need inside of me was too much to bear.

Wrapping my hand around the back of her thong, I shifted it to the side. I could feel her wetness all over my fingers. The fact that she was wet made me crazy.

"Fuck, Jade. I need to be inside of you. Tell me it's okay.

She kissed me and moaned into my mouth, "Please. Tyler, I want you so badly right now."

I couldn't believe what was about to happen. I was about to have my dream girl.

I was stiff to the point of pain and couldn't unbuckle my jeans fast enough, letting them fall to my ankles. This first time with her was hardly going to be graceful. I guess you could say it was a lot like our very first meeting, frantic and clumsy...but fucking amazing.

As tall as she was, she felt light as a feather as I lifted her up over my cock.

When I entered her, I closed my eyes. She felt so tight and wet. I needed a moment to relish how damn phenomenal it felt and also what it really meant. I knew wholeheartedly that I had just become one with the only woman I would ever need.

Jade was so ready for me. She closed her eyes in an almost hypnotic trance as she gyrated her hips over me.

I could have exploded inside of her at any second if I let myself. It took incredible resistance not to, because moving in and out of her was just about the best damn thing I had ever felt.

This was everything.

"You're so fucking beautiful, Jade," I said as I pumped harder.

She suddenly gasped, bending her head back and I could feel her tighten around me. Holy shit...two minutes into it, and she was coming. The most beautiful sounds of pleasure escaped her as her pussy clamored down over me.

My balls tightened, and I came so hard inside of her, catching the last of her orgasm pulsating around my cock. I kept fucking her until nothing was left in me.

She felt limp against me. Her mouth was buried in my neck as she said, "I'm sorry."

"Don't you dare apologize. That was so hot that you lost control," I said, pulling her over to the couch.

"I don't know what came over me."

"Well, *you* came over *me*."

"True."

We fell into a deep kiss, our naked and sated bodies still glued together as she straddled me.

Jade spoke over my lips. "How long can you stay?"

"I'm not going back."

She pulled away to look at me. "What?"

"You heard me. Did you not see that massive suitcase?"

"Are you serious? What about the play?"

"My understudy was over the moon for his big break— the director not so much. But it doesn't matter. You're more important than some community fucking theater performance. We can't make this work long distance."

"I can't believe you would do this for me. No man has ever sacrificed anything for me."

"Then, they couldn't have felt about you the way I do."

"What about your mother?"

"She'll be okay. She was really supportive. She's a romantic at heart. She's never gotten over my father. She didn't want me to live with the guilt of never having pursued this. Everything about home changed the moment you came into it and left. Nothing was the same. Everything before you is in the past. It doesn't exist. My future is here with you."

CHAPTER *eleven*

Jade

There was nothing like getting woken up by a smoking hot man moving in and out of you. My eyes might have been barely open, but I was wet as all hell and halfway to orgasm.

After we both came for what was probably the seventh time since Tyler walked through my door last night, we lay in a blissful state of quiet.

Tyler gently rubbed the side of my face as he spoke, "Something's on your mind."

Leaning my cheek into my palm, I asked. "Are you sure you thought this through?"

"I didn't need to. I would've come to the same conclusion no matter how much time I spent thinking it over. There was no choice to make."

"I'm supposed to be going back to work this week."

"And?"

"And I won't be able to spend time with you."

"I'm not needy, Jade. I have to find a damn job. I have plenty to do. You don't need to feel guilty. I'll more than make up for it when you're home. I'll rub your feet after a long day, or maybe rub your clit with my tongue, whatever method you prefer to relax. And if I don't get work right away, this place will be spotless and you'll have a hot meal and a glass of wine waiting for you every night."

"That sounds like heaven, but seriously, I feel guilty that you gave up your career for me."

"Listen…it's your time to shine, okay? You've already established a successful career. If it's meant to happen for me, it will. Right now, I just want to be with you. That's my priority."

It was my time to shine. Seriously? Was he for real? I had never been with someone so selfless.

"I want to try to hook you up with an acting gig," I insisted.

Tyler seemed adamant. "I won't take it. I refuse to ride on your coattails. That's not what I came here for. I'll go on auditions, but I'll get gigs based on merit."

I scratched his stubble. "I don't know what to do with you, Tyler Hennessey."

He took my hand and placed it on his rigid cock. "I'll give you plenty to do."

EPILOGUE

TWO YEARS LATER

Tyler

It was almost show time. I was backstage with Jade, relishing my final moments with her.

There wasn't one day that went by that I didn't thank my lucky stars that she had chosen me.

Life in New York hadn't been easy. My time, for the most part over the past couple of years, was been spent working odd jobs and auditioning in between. But the one constant was getting to sleep next to her every night. And that made it all worth it.

My fiancée was a natural born star. So, tonight was going to be a strange reversal.

"I'm so proud of you, Tyler. When you told me you wanted to start from scratch without my help, I thought you were crazy, but clearly, I should've never doubted you. Look at where we are."

I was starting to get the jitters. "Are you gonna be okay out there?"

"Yes. I might have to get up to go to the bathroom a few times, but I'll be fine. I'm so excited to see the show."

"Well, knowing that my two good luck charms will be out there on opening night is all the luck I'll need."

I knelt down to kiss her swollen belly. If I thought my woman was the most beautiful creature in the world before, she was even more beautiful pregnant.

Jade had to stop performing a few months ago when she really started to show. She'd be taking a year off from Broadway to stay home with our baby boy. It was what she wanted. Around the same time, I got the lead role in a new show, *The Vegas Project.* Everything was coming together like it had been written in the stars.

My dream to perform alongside her someday had yet to be realized. But I knew one day it would happen.

The stage manager made an announcement, which meant I had to leave her.

I pulled her close. "I love you, Jade."

"I love you, too, Tyler." She started to walk away then blew me one last kiss and said, "It's your time to shine, baby."

Want to read Tyler and Jade's first Christmas encounter from a different point of view? It was featured as part of my full-length STANDALONE novel, NEIGHBOR DEAREST (the love story of Chelsea and Damien). A *New York Times* bestseller.

ABOUT THE *author*

Penelope Ward is a *New York Times, USA Today* and #1 *Wall Street Journal* Bestselling author of thirteen novels. She is a fifteen-time *New York Times* Bestseller (hitting at the #2 spot on three separate occasions). Several of her books have been translated into foreign languages and can be found in bookstores around the world.

Penelope spent most of her twenties as a television news anchor before switching to a more family-friendly career. She grew up in Boston with five older brothers. She lives for reading books in the new adult genre, coffee, messaging with her buddy and sometimes co-author, Vi Keeland, as well as hanging out with her friends and family on weekends.

She is the proud mother of a beautiful 12-year-old girl with autism (the inspiration for the character Callie in Gemini) and a 10-year-old boy, both of whom are the lights of her life.

Penelope, her husband, and kids reside in Rhode Island.

Email Penelope at: penelopewardauthor@gmail.com
Newsletter Signup: http://bit.ly/1X725rj
Facebook Author Page: https://www.facebook.com/penelopewardauthor
Facebook Fan Group (Request to join!) https://www.facebook.com/groups/PenelopesPeeps/
Instagram: https://instagram.com/PenelopeWardAuthor
Twitter: https://twitter.com/PenelopeAuthor
Website: www.penelopewardauthor.com

Printed in Great Britain
by Amazon

76999811R00057